CARRIE AND THE CRAZY QUILT

by

Nelda Johnson Liebig

Midwest Traditions, Inc.
Mount Horeb, Wisconsin

Midwest Traditions, Inc. is a nonprofit organization working to help preserve a sense of place and tradition in American life.

For a catalog of books, write:

Midwest Traditions
P.O. Box 320
Mount Horeb, Wisconsin 53572 U.S.A.
or call 1-800-736-9189

Carrie and the Crazy Quilt
Copyright © 1996 Nelda Johnson Liebig

ISBN 1-883953-19-7

Library of Congress Cataloging-in-Publication Data

Liebig, Nelda Johnson, 1930-
    Carrie and the crazy quilt / Nelda Johnson Liebig.
        p.   cm.
    Summary: Carrie's faith in God helps her to overcome her fears during the Great Peshtigo Fire of 1871.
    ISBN 1-883953-19-7 (pbk. : alk. paper)
    1. Forest fires–Wisconsin–Peshtigo Region–Juvenile fiction. 2. Peshtigo (Wis.)–History–Juvenile fiction. [1. Forest fires– Wisconsin–Peshtigo Region–Fiction.   2. Peshtigo (Wis.)– History–Fiction.   3. Fear–Fiction.   4. German Americans– Fiction. 5. Christian life–Fiction.] I. Title.
    PZ7.L61643Car   1996
    {Fic}–dc21   96-29722
                                                             CIP
                                                             AC

DEDICATION

This book is dedicated to the memory of Reverend Peter Pernin who, by his courage and faith in God, rescued many lives the night of October 8, 1871, during a forest fire that destroyed the town of Peshtigo, and much of northeast Wisconsin.

Note: Most names in this story are fictitious, and any resemblance to persons living or dead is purely coincidental.

"Your life is like this quilt," Oma said. *"Each thing that happens is like a piece of crazy quilt. Some things are bad and don't make sense until God stitches them together to form patterns."*

"Amid these floating torches (logs) came a cow swimming along where the river was deep, its eyes wide with fear. Clinging to one of its horns was a young girl, Carrie Heidenworth...in the excitement she got beyond her depth. As she went under she reached out for something to cling to. The cow blundered by just then. She grasped one of its curving horns. Carrie hung on tight."

— Robert Wells, FIRE AT PESHTIGO

TABLE OF CONTENTS

Chapter 1 — *Found*

"**M**ama, here they come!" Carrie tucked her long blond hair behind her ears as she often did when she was excited.

Carrie's mother came running out of the cabin and peered down the narrow road that disappeared into the forest. Carrie cupped her hand to shade her eyes from the evening sun. "They found him! They're coming from the marsh."

Mama's hands shook as she twisted her apron. Worry lines on her forehead changed to a question. "Fritz — my baby — is he all right?"

"Yes, Mama. Look! He sees us and he's waving. So are Papa and Father Pernin. And three of the searchers are with them."

Kleine, Fritz's collie, raced past Carrie down the road. He jumped and barked with joy. His plumed tail wagged wildly. His master was home!

"O thank our *liebe Gott!*" Mama exclaimed with a long sigh. She almost always spoke German. Even after five years in America English was so hard for her to learn.

Carrie nodded and, she too, thanked their loving God for bringing her little brother home. When Father Pernin stopped for Fritz before dawn that morning he assured Mama they would be home by mid day. Fritz was always eager to go with Father Pernin when he was hunting pheasants or rabbits.

The men sat around the big table in the kitchen. As they drank mugs of Mama's good coffee Father Pernin explained.

"There we were, Mrs. Heidenworth — your Fritz and me. Hunting pheasants and enjoying the beauty of God's woods when, without warning, fire crawled through the underbrush towards us." He stopped and rubbed his big hands together. "We turned to escape by way of the old marsh, but there it was — more fire. And then before I could pick Fritz up and run we were standing in a circle of fire. I thought of stamping it out, but I knew I couldn't. I knelt to pray right there in the marsh which is almost dry and has been all summer. I asked God to help us."

Father Pernin looked across the table with a grateful look at the men. "Then — right then — you came out of the woods calling our names. It took you no time to beat a path for us. The boy and I walked out of that circle of fire without so much as our socks scorched.

Everyone was quiet. Fritz, exhausted from the long day, was sleeping peacefully, curled on Papa's lap.

Carrie, seated on a stool near the open door, remembered how excited Fritz had been about going hunting with Father Pernin. He woke her up three times in the night asking her if it was time to get up. She sighed. *What a pest!* She knew it was wrong to have such thoughts and she was truly grateful to God that he was safe. *But, God, you know it's true. He's a pest.* Ever since that high fever two years ago when he was four years old. Mama explained that because of his sickness he would never be able to go to school or learn to read. But he could work on the homestead. And there was always so much to do.

Papa ran his hand across Fritz's blond curls. "Yes, when we came over the rise looking for you, we saw that fire. I tell you my heart stopped." He sighed. "The fires! When will they burn out? So tinder dry in the woods now. If only God would send rain."

Carrie felt as though her heart stopped too. She could hardly turn to look out the doorway. Would she see that fire creeping silently until, with a monstrous roar like a monstrous bear, it gobbled up the cabin? She shivered and hugged herself.

"Carrie," Mama said, "Wash now and go to bed. Tomorrow is the Sabbath and we must be up early to go to town."

Father Pernin stood and stretched. "Yes. I must go. Much to do before morning."

It seemed to Carrie that Father Pernin could almost touch the slanted roof with his finger tips as his long arms reached above his head. He didn't seem much like a priest. Some people said he had been a lumberjack before God called him to be a minister. But Papa said he was just a very strong man with a very strong faith in God.

Carrie washed in the lean-to shed connected to the kitchen, then climbed the ladder to the sleeping loft. Even though she wasn't cold she snuggled under her crazy quilt, the one she and

Oma made together three years ago. She listened as the men talked about the fires and what to do if their homesteads were in danger.

Carrie shivered and put her head under her quilt so she wouldn't hear them.

Chapter 2 – *More Danger in the Woods*

 "**C**arrie! Carrie Hildegard Heidenworth!"

Carrie came running out of the cabin tying her bonnet over her long blond hair. She hurried to the wagon.

"The door, Carrie!" Papa said firmly.

"Oh, yes." She whirled around, pushed the heavy door shut, then dropped the wooden bar in place. No one would break in, but one of the cows might walk right in and make herself at home. Carrie grinned at the thought of her black and white Hildy sitting at the table having a bowl of cornmeal mush.

"I'm sorry Papa. I couldn't find my bonnet." She scrambled up the wheel spokes and sat next to Fritz. She gathered her dress close to her on the old blanket Papa had spread out to protect their Sunday clothes.

Mama and Papa sat tall on the wagon seat, eyes straight ahead as the team responded to Papa's clucking. With a slap of the reins across their rumps the horses started down the lane and out on to the dusty road that led to the village of Peshtigo.

Smoke! thought Carrie, looking around. Always smoke! And ashes! She brushed at the ashes on her dark green dress. She clamped a hand over her nose and closed her eyes. Won't the fires ever stop?

Papa said the settlers burning stumps to clear their land had caused the fires. Others claimed that sparks from the locomotives pulling loads of logs were to blame. But nothing could spoil this day for Carrie. *My birthday! October 1, 1871 and I'm 13 years old. Best of all Lisa is coming home with me after church.*

Carrie watched the cabin until it was out of sight among the tall pines as the wagon turned a bend in the road. She thought about the log cabin Papa and neighbors had built. Five years ago when they homesteaded here in Wisconsin. That's how it was, everyone helping each other to build before winter.

"Papa," she called. "Tell us again what the homestead claim means."

"Well, now," he replied with a broad smile partly hidden by his black mustache, "we got one hundred sixty acres from the government. Then we began clearing and planting it. Now, after five years of improving it, we have our deed of ownership." He looked at Mama and his shoulders straightened with pride. "The Herman Heidenworth farm."

There was a proud ring to his voice and Carrie knew he never tired of telling that story, just like she never tired of hearing it.

"We will have a fine dairy farm some day."
Then he added softly, "No more making axe
handles and buckets at the woodenware factory
for me."

Carrie knew she should be proud and happy.
They had accomplished so much in five years. The
cabin, the shed, the barn. And the root cellar in
the side of the hill behind the tool shed. But would
she ever get over her fear of the deep woods? And
the night sounds were scariest of all.

Fritz stood on his knees and looked back down
the road. "Here he comes! Come on, Kleine!" He
laughed and clapped his hands as the dog caught
up with the wagon in a few long strides then trotted along just ahead of the team.

Kleine always escorted his family to church.
The big wagon never left the farm without Kleine.
He knew it was his job to be with his family.

At the church, the big collie would sit under
the wagon keeping watch through the two hour
service. When there were church dinners after services, Kleine waited eagerly for the food scraps
that Fritz brought him. Then he stretched his full
length and slept until the singing and activities
were over. At last he could take his family back
home along the banks of the Peshtigo river. Back
to the farm three miles south of the village.

"Mama," called Carrie from the back of the
wagon. "May Lisa and I swim in Blue Hole this
afternoon?"

Mama thought a minute. "What do you think
Herman?"

"Well, it's beastly hot," Papa replied, "And it is your birthday. You must observe the quiet of the Sabbath."

"Yes, Papa." She paused. "And please, Mama, may we have a picnic lunch?"

Mama nodded as she held her handkerchief over her mouth and nose. A bank of gray smoke drifted down over them.

"Me, too, I want a picnic too." Fritz jumped up.

"Sit down, son," Papa said firmly.

Carrie shook her head and frowned at Fritz, but before she could tell him he couldn't go, Mama said, "Of course you can go. It's your sister's birthday."

Why does he always have to come? Carrie thought. He's such a *feigling*. She bit her lip. Who was she to call anyone a coward? She was the biggest one of all. And she thought about his sickness. The doctor had even said he wouldn't live.

Smoke rolled thick and sour. Carrie covered her face with the hem of her dress.

Now the wagon bumped along by the new school. A boy was picking up lumber scraps from the yard. The new school looked so important. Carrie was proud she was a student there.

"That's Hans Heiss. And working on the Sabbath," she mumbled to herself. "Probably being punished for some stupid thing he did." She knew Hans didn't go to church—probably didn't even believe in God.

Much too tall for the gray homespun pants that ended just below his knees Hans loaded his arms with wood and dumped it in a pile at the edge of the road. His hair hung in his eyes. Tipping his head back to see, he called and waved. "Hi, Carrie!" But she turned away so she wouldn't have to look at him.

Miss Moore assigned Hans the biggest seat at the back of the room because he had to put his long legs out in the aisle. It seemed to Carrie they were always in the way when she had to go to the cloak room to get something for Miss Moore. And everyone knew Miss Moore also put him at the back because he was a trouble-maker. Or at least he would be, but Miss Moore could manage him even though he was 15 years old. She could discipline all forty students in the room. Yes. Everyone was afraid of Miss Moore.

Why would Hans call to me anyway? She clenched her fists. *That awful bully!* She would never forget the time he grabbed Lisa's lunch bucket and ate her bread-and-butter sandwich. Then he threw the bucket in the bushes. Lisa had tried not to cry, but her lip trembled. The other kids laughed. Even though Carrie was afraid of Hans towering over her she drew back her own bucket and whopped him on the back. He took off through the woods. No one was more surprised than Carrie.

When she got home and had to explain the dent in her bucket Mama reminded her she should settle problems by talking. She would never forget Mama's words, "Remember, Carrie, you have God on your side, and He expects you to be a peacemaker."

But her grandmother added, "Yes, try to work things out with words, but when that fails a lunch bucket will do just fine." Then she chuckled and turned back to her mending.

"*Oma!*" Even though Carrie worked hard at using English instead of her native German, she always called her grandmother by the German pet name for Grandma. Mama and Papa were strict about her using English. But sometimes she forgot, especially if she got excited.

The wagon bumped up on to the village bridge. Carrie clutched the sideboards. Oh, how the wagon shook her bones.

From the middle of the bridge she could see the whole village along both sides of the river. And six blocks ahead along the wooden side walk stood her new church still being built. The half-finished spire stood high above the trees in a halo of smoke.

She usually liked coming to the village. But this morning was different. The smoke! Thick and sour smelling. Over the houses, stores, the black-smith shop, the saw mill and the woodenware factory. And the air was hotter, much hotter, than out on the homestead. Suddenly she didn't want to be here. Not at all. But, oh, she did want to see Lisa.

And Lisa is coming to the farm today — for my birthday!

*Chapter 3 – **Fire!***

At the church Carrie jumped down from the wagon and ran toward the door eager to find Lisa Zutter. But Mama called, "Caroline!"

Carrie stopped. How could she have forgotten again? No running on the Sabbath. "I'm sorry, Mama."

Mama sighed. "Now smooth your hair and try to act like a lady."

The last thing Carrie wanted to do was to act like a lady, but she tucked strands of her sunbleached hair behind her ears and ran her fingers down her part. It was straight — well, sort of straight. She combed her shoulder length hair with her fingers. "Who cares in this heat?" she thought.

In the church the air was cooler and almost free of smoke. Carrie loved the smell of new wood.

"Still no pews," Mama said, looking around at the empty church.

Papa nodded. "Ja! Zutter will be plastering in a week or so," he replied in German.

Carrie knew Papa was excited when he spoke only German. Usually it was a scramble of English and German together. And sometimes that could sound very funny.

"And after the plastering," Papa continued, "the men of the church will put the pews in. *Ja*, our new church building will soon be finished. And a fine one, too."

Carrie sat next to Mama on a rough plank placed across two big logs. Soon the room was almost full of worshippers. Carrie knew some, but many were new in town. Peshtigo was growing very fast. Men were coming to work in the giant woodenware factory where Papa was employed.

Mr. and Mrs. Zahn and their new baby sat in front of the Heidenworth family. Carrie remembered with pride the crazy quilt she and Oma made last year for the raffle to raise money for the new church. Oh, the look on Frieda Zahn's face when she won that pretty quilt. The hodge-podge pieces zig-zagged every which way creating their own design. But Carrie still loved the old one on her bed in the loft at home best.

Father Pernin entered through a side door near the pulpit. The legs of his coarse trousers and the collar of a shabby shirt were all that could be seen of his clothing. The rest of the priest was covered by his black robe. Carrie wondered why he wasn't wearing his black suit under his robe as he always did. She was glad he wore a robe for services. Without it he didn't look much like a priest.

"Good morning." He greeted his congregation in his heavy French accent.

When he arrived in Peshtigo last year Papa had grumbled about having a French priest for the congregation. But Mama had scolded him. "Now Herman Heidenworth. What if the church forbade Germans here? Where would *we* be?"

Carrie thought she could twist around just enough to look for Lisa, but with the first wiggle Mama's eyes were on her. So she stared at an interesting knot hole in the floor. It looked like a hawk's eye. She shivered. She didn't like the hawks that perched in the trees over the chicken pen waiting to catch some of Mama's young chicks.

Carrie glanced over at her mother in her soft blue silk dress. In the trunk at the foot of Mama and Papa's bed she had two more elegant dresses adorned with lace and ribbons. Mama looked so fine in them. She and Papa brought them from Stuttgart in Germany, where she grew up in Grandfather Werner and Oma's pretty little house. Now that house was only a picture above the fireplace in the cabin.

Carrie sighed. "Oh, Grandfather, you went to heaven while we were still in Germany and now Oma has gone there, too. I miss you."

Suddenly the sawmill whistle began to shriek. The sound echoed throughout the village. People around Carrie turned to peer out the windows. Some stood and looked out the door.

"Ach! What's wrong?" Carrie whispered to Mama.

Before her mother could reply a mill worker came striding down the aisle, his boots clumping on the new floor."Fire! Fire!" Carrie clamped her hand over her mouth to keep from crying out.

"Sorry, Father Pernin!" The man ran his fingers through his carrot orange hair and looked around at the men. "Fires are breaking out in the underbrush across the river. We need more help."

Father Pernin nodded, then prayed a short prayer. After the "Amen" all the men and boys who were able to fight the fire jumped up and rushed for the door.

Carrie squeezed her hands together, her breath coming in little jerks. A woman behind her began to sob.

"O God our Creator," prayed Father Pernin, "protect those who fight the fires. Give them strength to subdue it. Amen." He opened the big pulpit Bible and read:

Fear not, for I have redeemed you; I have summoned you by name, you are mine. When you pass through waters, I will be with you; and when you pass through the rivers, they will not sweep over you. When you walk through the fire, you will not be burned; the flames will not set you ablaze. *

Then Father Pernin closed the Bible and dismissed the congregation. With several long steps he was at the door tossing his long black robe on a box. Then he was gone to help fight the fires.

---

* Isaiah 43:1-2 KJV

Now Carrie understood why he had on old clothes under his robe.

"Lisa!" Carrie hurried to her friend.

"Kate, thank you for taking Lisa with you today," said Mrs. Zutter. "I'm going to Marinette. My mother is ill again."

"I'm so sorry, Mertie." Mama patted the woman's arm. "Now, don't you worry about Lisa. She can walk to school with Carrie in the morning."

Carrie and Lisa scooped up their long skirts and scrambled up into the wagon. They sat on the blanket in the far back. "I just know something awful is going to happen," Lisa whispered.

Fritz sat close to Mama. "Mama, can you make the horses go like Papa does?" He looked up at her fearfully.

She gave a light rap of the reins. "Don't worry. I won't have any trouble driving the team. They are as eager as we are to get back to the farm."

Heads up, ears perked, the horses trotted down the street and over the bridge. With a sharp turn south they were on the road to the homestead.

Fritz looked around for his dog. Kleine dashed ahead, stopping only to glance back to see that his family was coming along behind him.

Chapter 4 – *The Birthday Gift*

Carrie and Lisa swung the picnic basket between them. Boiled eggs, thick bread and butter sandwiches and sweet spiced applesauce lay wrapped in one of Mama's clean dishcloth. Fritz carried a jug of cool water fresh from the well.

They spread the picnic blanket on the bank of the creek near Blue Hole. The cabin was just across the potato field, but to Carrie this was another world — her world.

Fritz stood rubbing his eyes.

"Don't do that," Carrie scolded. "It makes them sting worse. Here, sit down. The smoke isn't as bad near the ground."

Fritz flopped down, and Kleine stretched out beside him.

Lisa reached in her pocket. "Happy birthday!" She handed Carrie a piece of carved wood with a leather cord strung through a hole in it.

Carrie frowned. "It's half of a circle with parts of words on it. Is it broken?"

"No." Lisa laughed. "See." She took the other half from her pocket. She held it next to Carrie's. "FRIENDS FOREVER," Lisa read. "You wear half and I wear half."

"You carved them! And polished them. Oh, Lisa, I'll never take it off." Carrie slipped the leather string over her head.

Soon the food was all gone. "Come on, Lisa, I'll race you." It wasn't much of a race. Lisa's short legs were no match for Carrie's long strides along the creek bank.

"Oh, no," Carrie moaned as she splashed giant steps into the water. "The water is only up to my knees."

"Ach!" Lisa frowned. She squatted down and ran her fingers through the water.

"Let's wade to Bear Rock," said Carrie. They threw their skirts over a tree limb, then pulled their bloomers above their knees. "Oooh, it feels so good!" Carrie sat down and let the cool water flow over her legs.

Lisa waded, but didn't get very wet. Kleine joined them, jumping and barking. Fritz watched from the shade of a bush.

The short October daylight was fading. And Carrie's birthday with it. They started back to the cabin.

"Let's go sit in the cool cellar," suggested Lisa.

"Tell Mama where we are, Fritz," said Carrie. "And when Papa gets home, come and get us."

Lisa pulled the door shut behind them and sat on the cool hard packed dirt floor in the darkness. They took deep breaths of the cool clean air! Suddenly Carrie reached over and pushed the door open to welcome a streak of light.

"No need to sit in the dark," she said. "Can't see you." She picked up a potato, rubbed it clean on her skirt and began to munch on it.

"I know," Lisa said softly, sharing Carrie's secret. "You are afraid of the dark. Just like I'm scared of water."

Carrie thought only Oma knew how darkness grabbed at her. How it squeezed the breath out of her. "You can't be as afraid of anything as I am of the dark." Carrie covered her face, ashamed to let Lisa know.

"Yes, I can. Even though I swam with you all the way to the big tree last summer, I kept my eyes shut tight and swam as fast as I could just to grab that tree."

Lisa's fears seemed small to Carrie. "Why am I such a *feigling*, Lisa? Yes, a big coward. I can't even sit in the dark cellar. Even Fritz can, and he's my little brother."

"Carrie," Lisa whispered as though the earth walls had listening ears. "Let's promise never to tell anyone else how scared we are." She reached for Carrie's hand. "Promise?"

Carrie nodded. "I'm three years older than you. Yet I'm more afraid of lots of things than you could ever be." She got up and pushed the door open. "Let's go."

"Wait." Lisa tugged at Carrie's arm. "I'm supposed to tell you something. But I couldn't until Fritz left."

Carrie pushed the door wider. The smoky evening light shone on Lisa's face. "Well, what is it?"

"Uh..." Lisa stammered. "A boy asked me to tell you that he likes you."

"Quit teasing," Carrie snapped.

"I'm not teasing. It's—it's Hans. He wants to talk to you."

"Hans? That bully? That—that sandwich stealer. Never!"

As they left the cellar Carrie pushed the door tight against the hillside to keep any animals out. As they approached the cabin Papa was coming down the road. His shoulders sagged with weariness. His face was smeared with soot.

Carrie hoped the fires were out. That should make her feel better. But it didn't. Fear grabbed at her stomach.

Chapter 5 — *A Strange October*

Carrie sat on a stump on the bank of the creek behind the barn. She ran her fingers over the letters on the wooden tombstone Papa had carved last month.

CAROLINE HILDEGARD HEIDENWORTH
BORN 1805   DIED 1871

Carrie was glad she was named after her grandmother. But she wished Papa had carved the word *Oma* on it.

"Ach! How I miss you, Oma," she whispered. "If you were here, I wouldn't be so afraid. And you know Fritz, he cries in his sleep more than ever before."

She looked up at the blanket of gray smoke hanging over the homestead. She brushed at her arm. Ashes! Would she ever feel clean again? She wished Lisa could be here today. They'd go to the creek, just like last Sunday. She touched her necklace. Then she pushed her hair out of her eyes and tucked it behind her ears. It was streaked with gray even though she washed it every day. Ashes drifted down over her. "*Seltsam!*" she cried. "Yes! Strange! This is the strangest October ever!"

"Carrie," Mama called. "Did you get the cows as you were told?"

Carrie jumped up from the stump. "I'm going, Mama." She started along the creek, her bare feet making little puffs of dust and ashes.

"Wait for me," yelled Fritz, trying to catch her.

"Hurry up!" she snapped.

"Why were you sitting by Oma's grave, Carrie?"

She was quiet for a minute. "Because I miss her. I want to talk to her like when we sat near the fireplace on dark winter days."

"But she's gone."

Carrie nodded. She wondered how much he understood about death. She knew she didn't understand it. "We will see her in Heaven some day." The lump in her throat grew bigger.

"Where's Heaven?" His large blue eyes searched her face. He waited, believing his sister knew the answers to all of his questions. His thick blond curls, now stiff with soot, framed his thin face. "Is she up there?" He pointed toward the sky with a soot smudged finger.

Carrie coughed and put her hand over her mouth and nose. A light breeze brought a weaving line of smoke.

Suddenly Fritz grabbed her hand and began to cry.

She squeezed his sweaty palm. "Now try not to be afraid." She hoped she sounded brave. "Papa said the fires should burn out soon. Winter is coming. And Christmas!" She wanted to sound excited, but the words came out flat.

"Mama told you to get the cows in the barn."

"Don't I know that?" *Why did he always remind her?* "Papa said if the fires come closer the livestock could run away. Now where is that dog when we need him? Kleine! Come!"

The soot covered collie crawled from under the buggy next to the barn. He sniffed the air and whimpered before returning to the cooler air under the rig.

"Kleine! *Kommen Sie hier!*" Carrie yelled. She squatted by the buggy peering under it. "I said come here!"

The dog's long nose appeared but he just looked out at her. "What a dumb name for him."

"Why?" asked Fritz, lying on his stomach, looking at Kleine.

"Why? Because he is so big. That's why. It's silly to call him *Little One*. He's bigger than a spring calf."

Spring! What a beautiful word, she thought, as she stood up and brushed dirt and soot from her skirt.

It was spring when they moved into the two room cabin. It seemed so big after living in the tent that smelled like moldy bread. Flowering shrubs filled the woods then. Next, the barn was built. And during the long summer evenings the root cellar was dug in the hill. Just in time for the vegetables to be stored.

The rocky ground had to be cleared before Papa could plow. Carrie hated picking rocks more than any other chore on the farm. Back and forth the family walked, putting stones of all sizes into the stone boat which was a sled pulled by one of the horses. The rocks made a fence around Mama's garden. There would be more stones and more fences every year.

"Carrie, get the cows," Fritz whined.

"Oh, I'm going!" Carrie ran across the field calling, "Trudy! Babe! Hildy!"

Fritz stumbled along behind her. "Don't leave me!"

he cows stood in a deeper part of the creek near Blue Hole. It was normally clear, cool and inviting to them. Now it wasn't much more than a mud hole.

Carrie swished one foot in the water. She could almost hear Oma's laughter. How many times had they waded together here looking for pretty pebbles to add to the jar on the fireplace mantel?

Even though Oma had been old, she could step lightly over the large smooth rocks that were so plentiful in the creek. She was the only person Carrie could talk to about things that scared her. She even told Oma about the strange noises in the cabin.

"I pull my crazy quilt over my head," she told Oma one day as they sat near this very spot. "Even on hot nights when I hear things."

"Now, Carrie! That's only the mice getting settled for the winter. They nest near the stone chimney by your bed. It's warm and safe for them.

Remember, they are God's creatures, too, Carrie, my *Liebling.*"

"*Liebling,*" Carrie said, as she sat on a fallen tree, dangling her feet in the creek.

"What?" asked Fritz, crawling slowly out on the tree to be near her.

"Ach! I was just thinking about Oma. Remember how she called me her *Liebling?*" It's true. I was her pet. Oh, she loved you too, Fritz. Very much. But she thought of me sort of like I think of my Hildy. My pet ever since she was born." Carrie swished her toes in the water.

"Get the cows!" Fritz backed off the drooping tree. He trudged along the creek bank toward the three cows who eyed him suspiciously.

Smoke hung thick over the water giving it the color of clay. Now Blue Hole was less than four feet deep in the middle and the rest of the creek bed was almost dry. The cool water tickled her legs. Today was even hotter than last Sunday when Lisa was with them. "Fritz! Let's wade."

He shook his head. "Get the cows, Carrie."

She tossed her skirt and petticoat over a log. The wide ruffle on her petticoat dangled in the water. She tucked her blouse in her bloomers which were made from one of Oma's kitchen aprons. She was sure Oma didn't need aprons in Heaven. She waded out to Bear Rock. Again, she wished Lisa was here.

"Caroline Hildegard Heidenworth!" Mama's voice carried all the way across the potato field.

"Mama is mad," Fritz warned.

Carrie knew Mama was truly angry when she called her by her full name. She scrambled out of the creek. She flapped her skirt and petticoat as she moved toward Hildy who had followed her. The cow lowered her head, let out a bawl and backed away.

"What's the matter with you, girl?" Carrie took another step toward her. "Now you go to the barn," she said firmly. She remembered Hildy as the skinny calf on wobbly legs. Her white pet with black splotches—or was she black with white spots? Her funny little beggar who came to the back door for handouts. But now she was two years old and stood as tall as Carrie.

Hildy tossed her head and rolled her large brown eyes. She watched Carrie flapping the skirt near her.

Anger flew all over Carrie. "Move!" Suddenly she felt awful yelling at Hildy like that. She reached out to stroke the broad soft nose. But Hildy backed away again. Then suddenly that cow lowered her head swinging it slowly from side to side, horns aimed straight at Carrie. Carrie had never seen her like this. She dropped her petticoat and backed slowly away.

But with a loud bellow Hildy came at her.

Carrie scrambled to the middle of the creek. Now the other cows were coming, too. Their large curved horns seemed bigger with each step. Carrie screamed and splashed. Then she screamed louder. The cows stopped and bawled. Their huge eyes grew even wilder.

Fritz crouched behind a tree, too terrified to cry.

Papa came running across the clearing, his leather boots thumping the hard plowed ground.

He waved his sweat-stained hat at the cows until they turned away.

Carrie tried not to cry. "Papa, what's wrong with them?" With shaking hands she put on her petticoat and skirt.

"Frightened," he answered, "never know how animals will act when they suspect danger."

"Danger? They're afraid of *me*?"

He scanned the sky with a worried look. "No, not you, Carrie. The fires. Come. Mama wants you to go to Father Pernin's."

Fritz rubbed at his tears, smearing soot around his eyes, giving him a raccoon look. "What about the cows?" he asked.

"I'll get them later, son."

Carrie hoped Papa couldn't feel her tremble as she snuggled against him. If only she could stay close to him, maybe things would be all right. Maybe the fear that squeezed her heart would go away.

Chapter 7 – *Where Will We Go?*

Carrie, Fritz and Papa crossed the potato field, which was all brown and lumpy from last week's digging. Carrie knew Mama would be upset about her muddy skirt and for having to tell her a dozen times to bring the cows.

Carrie knew, too, it was wrong not to mind right away. She always had other things on her mind when there was work to be done. She would tell Mama how sorry she was, and then do some extra work. Mama worked so hard, and now she didn't have Oma to help her any more.

Papa got a bucket. They picked up a few potatoes that had been missed when the family dug hundreds of them last week. They put them in the cellar. The smells in the dark cool room greeted them.

Papa ducked to keep from bumping into clusters of onions tied to the rafters. Carrie stayed in the open doorway as Papa and Fritz put the potatoes on the wooden racks. There would be food for the winter. But the crop was poor after only one day of rain all summer. There were turnips, carrots, cabbages and rutabagas on racks made of criss-crossed layers of small tree limbs. It was Carrie and Fritz's job to have enough racks for the vegetables.

She thought of Lisa and the promise they made here last Sunday. Carrie touched her necklace. She hadn't taken it off since Lisa gave it to her. She knew Lisa would keep her promise not to tell anybody about their fears.

A purple velvet blanket of smoke floated over the potato field as Papa closed the cellar door. Outside of the cool cellar the air felt like the heat of the big black oven when Carrie took out Mama's sweet smelling bread. It had been two years since there had been a cool summer day, a normal day for northern Wisconsin.

"Papa," Fritz asked, looking up at him, "will the fire burn us?" He stumbled over a bucket-sized clod of dirt and fell. Papa scooped him up and balanced him on one hip and pulled Carrie close with a tight hug that surprised Carrie. Papa wasn't one to show his feelings.

"Son, if it gets bad, it could burn the farm. But we will fight it, won't we?"

Carrie knew Papa would always be honest with them. He was strict about telling the truth. He wouldn't even allow books of make-believe stories like Aesop's Fables in the house. He would say, "We must always speak and read the truth as God would have us do."

And Carrie knew there could be no argument. Was she wrong to dream about make-believe things? Stories came in her head without her thinking about them.

An orange glow swelled above the forest to the west. Then it faded. Heavy smoke once again controlled the sky.

"Will God burn our house?" Fritz asked.

"It isn't God's fault, is it, Papa?" Carrie asked.

"No. We can't blame Him. Homesteaders have to burn stumps. Our land is cleared one stump at a time. That starts fires if we aren't careful. And locomotives shower the woods with sparks."

"Why don't they stop coming in the woods?" Carrie demanded.

"Then how would we get the timber out to cities where it is needed?" Papa often answered a question with one of his own.

"What will we do if the fire comes?" Carrie couldn't stop asking questions even though her throat tightened with fear.

"We'll take blankets and go to Blue Hole."

"Blankets?" Fritz looked up at Papa, his face a question mark.

"That's right, son. Cover ourselves with wet blankets and be brave, no matter what happens."

Carrie realized he had been thinking about it. Yes, Papa had a plan. She only wished it made her feel safe. *Ach!* If only Papa knew how much she wanted to be brave.

"Remember, *der liebe Gott* is with us."

Yes, Carrie knew it was true. The good Lord was with them. But why didn't that make her feel safe?"

"No matter what happens," Papa continued, "you must be brave. And now that's enough talk about fire. Fritz, turn the potatoes in the cellar to-morrow. Must keep them from rotting." He walked faster. *"Mitkommen! Come along.* Mama will be worried."

Carrie took long steps to keep up. Papa trusted God for everything, she thought, especially work at the woodenware factory. He was proud to work there. It was the largest in the state. And it was good pay. But he would quit someday and clear the south acres of the homestead. They would be full-time farmers, like Papa always said. And he loved his woodcrafting too. She thought of his tool chest. He would build fine furniture. That chest had been the most important part of their baggage on the boat when they came to America. Yes, someday there would be a big house built by Papa, standing near the road to the village.

Chapter 8 — *A Seltsam Wind*

Mama wiped her hands on her apron, which was stained with blackberry juice. Her face went dark at the sight of her daughter, looking nothing like the neat slender girl who left the cabin a few hours ago.

Carrie's honey-colored hair, now in tangles, almost covered her sunburned cheeks. Instead of braids as her mother liked, Carrie always pleaded to have it hang loose down her back.

"Please, Mama," she would beg, "I want to feel the breeze blowing through my hair." But there had been no cool breeze all summer.

"What am I to do with you, Caroline Hildegard?"

"Now, Kate." Papa put Fritz down and held up his calloused hands as though surrendering. "There is more to this than you see. Our Carrie girl does love the water."

Carrie saw the mischief in Papa's eyes. She squirmed inside. He rarely teased. And she wished he wouldn't tease now. She understood him better when he was stern.

Carrie pulled her hair behind her ears. "Oh, Mama, I am sorry, truly sorry."

Mama sighed. "I have a blackberry pie, venison stew, butter, and fresh bread for Father Pernin. I know he needs the food. His housekeeper is a good worker, but she can't cook."

"But Kate," said Papa, "You don't cook French food."

"Food is food." Mama frowned. "Besides, he doesn't need all those sweets and fluffy things. A big man needs hearty fare."

Carrie climbed the ladder to the sleeping loft.

"And hurry home," Mama added. "You know how difficult it is to see along the road in the dark."

"She won't have trouble seeing the road," said Papa, standing in the doorway.

The sound in his voice made Carrie stop on the ladder and look. "*Seltsam!*" she whispered. Across the road tongues of fire lapped hungrily at the tinder-dry grass and underbrush.

Mama hurried to the door. With a gasp she clapped her hands to her cheeks, but said nothing.

"Now, Kate, the fire that broke out last Sunday across the river was worse than this. We put it out in a few hours. If we're in danger Jake Mueller's boys will help trench around the buildings and beat out any small fires that break out."

His voice was calm but Carrie saw the look he gave Mama.

Fear sucked the breath out of Carrie. Her legs went limp. She could hardly pull herself up the ladder to the loft. She changed into her other homespun skirt. She brushed soot from her old crazy quilt on her bed before she sat on it. She ran her fingers over the patches put together every which way. She thought of the evenings she and Oma worked on it when she was only ten. The little scraps from Oma's sewing basket didn't look like much until they were all one quilt.

"Your life is like this quilt," Oma said. "Each thing that happens is like a piece of crazy-quilt. Some things are bad and don't make sense, until God stitches them together to form patterns."

"You mean like this patch I can't make fit together with any others?" Carrie asked.

Now, still sitting on her bed, Carrie brushed the quilt again and looked for that troublesome patch she had to redo, but she couldn't find it.

"Carrie!" Mama stood at the foot of the ladder. "Are you changed?"

"Yes, Mama, I'm coming — right now. "

"Fritz, you help carry the food," Papa said.

"I don't want to go." He clung to Mama's skirt.

"Don't be such a baby!" Carrie snapped, as she backed down the ladder. As soon as the words were out she was sorry. She lowered her voice. "Please, I need your help, little bruder. Maybe we will see Lisa." She helped Mama wrap the food in clean dish towels.

Fritz went to get Kleine from under the buggy.

"Tell Father Pernin he is welcome to come here," Mama said, wiping her hands on her apron. She wiped her hands again even though they didn't need it. She talked faster and kept looking out at the fires. "Fritz," she called out the window, "can't you find Kleine?"

Carrie liked to go to the church. Father Pernin was easy to talk with even with his thick French accent. He told such good stories. Carrie felt close to God when she was in the quiet church. She thought of the soldiers killing Jesus on a cross. She had asked Father Pernin why God didn't stop them.

"Don't question God's ways, child. We must not blame God for bad things that happen."

Carrie tucked a clean dish cloth over the food in the basket.

The clock on the fireplace mantel struck five. "Time to be on your way," Papa said.

The flames across the road danced up and down the ditch.

"Now don't stop for anything," Mama warned. She handed Fritz the loaf of bread wrapped tightly in a large linen napkin.

"Come on, Kleine," Fritz said. "We're going to town."

Kleine inched along behind Fritz. The long hairs on his hind legs, usually as fluffy as feathers, were stiff with gray ash. His big paws stirred up puffs of dust with every step. Suddenly he stopped. He sniffed the air and growled. He circled Fritz, then grabbed his pant leg in his teeth.

"Now stop that, Kleine!" Carrie commanded.

"He doesn't want to go, either," Fritz said.

Suddenly Kleine let go. He turned back toward the house. He stopped and barked at Fritz and Carrie. Then he began to whimper, his nose turned skyward.

Carrie felt sharp pains in her stomach as she watched him. She wanted to run back, too. She wanted to hug Mama and Papa and tell them she loved them. She looked down the smoky road. "Come on, Fritz." She reached for his hand. "Let's hurry."

Chapter 9 — To Town

Carrie clutched the basket with one hand as Fritz clung to the other. Wild daises at the edge of the wagon road drooped, bent over with ashes and dust. It was more like August in the north woods of Wisconsin rather than early October.

Twilight, all orange and red, filtered through the smoke haze all around Carrie and Fritz. He turned again and again to see if Kleine was on the road behind them.

"Why isn't he coming with us? He always comes." It was true. Kleine never let the family leave the homestead without him.

"It's all right, Fritz." Carrie hoped she sounded sure of herself. "Say! Did you know that the woodenware factory where Papa works is the largest in all of Wisconsin? Some day Peshtigo will be the most important city in the state." She paused. "Did you know that, Fritz? It's true. Papa said so." She wondered if Fritz knew she was just trying to keep him from thinking about Kleine and the fires.

She shifted the basket, careful not to tip the pie. As they neared the school she wondered how long it took Hans Heiss to pick up all those wood chips and scrap lumber. She was sure he deserved his punishment. Big bully! She looked around hoping he wasn't here now. She held the basket tighter as though she might have to smack him with it just like she did with her lunch bucket. Lisa said he wanted to talk to her. *Why?*

She could almost smell the clean new wood of the walls and benches in the school. She had the best seat, right next to one of the tall windows. And Lisa sat next to her.

The school was already crowded and more families arrived every week to work in the mill and factory. Even with forty in the room, Miss Moore could manage. Her dark eyes narrowed and a sharp line wrinkled her forehead when anyone started to make trouble. She stared in a way that made Carrie shiver. Carrie always kept her eyes on her work and didn't look at Miss Moore.

Even though Carrie got up early for school, sometimes her thoughts wandered and she would be late. Then she would run to school, her hair flying behind her. Miss Moore would be in the yard swinging the hand bell. Then Carrie would be in serious trouble.

"I want Kleine—and I'm tired," Fritz whined. "I don't want to go." He pulled at Carrie's hand.

"Let's stop here in the school yard and rest," she replied. "Look at that big crate." She put the basket down. They peeked between the boards.

"It's the new bell. It will be heard all the way to the homestead as soon as the men put it on the top of that post." She sighed. "Maybe it will help me be on time."

She remembered the morning Miss Moore gave her extra memory work for being late, then snapped, "Caroline! Stay in the real world."

Miss Moore even talked to Mama and Papa at church one Sunday. "Your daughter leaps in and out of daydreams like most of my students leap rocks in the Peshtigo river." Then she added sternly, "I will not have it!"

Carrie shuddered at the thought of Miss Moore's voice. She shifted the basket again. It felt heavier and the handle made a red mark on her arm. "Come on, let's get this food to Father Pernin."

Fritz continued to look for Kleine as they walked by the two-story boarding house where the unmarried mill workers lived. "See, that's where Papa works." Carrie pointed to the woodenware factory ahead of them. She was glad no one worked on Sunday. She hated the noise.

She didn't like mill noises at all. But she didn't like the eerie things that happened at home either. She tried not to think of the day she found bear tracks around the barn. She had run to the cabin, sure that bear was behind her. She even scrambled up the ladder and pulled her crazy quilt over her head. Oh, she was glad no one knew about that. Not even Oma.

As she and Fritz started across the town bridge near the sawmill, a hitch of six horses pulling a long wagon load of lumber clattered up the planks. Carrie pulled Fritz over to the railing to let it pass. The dark cold river below them flowed silently toward the dam carrying logs for the sawmill.

"See the big saw," she told Fritz, pointing to the open side of the mill. The giant blade stood taller than a man. On work days the whine of the saw echoed over the river as it sliced through a huge log. Today it was quiet.

Now the wagon load of logs cleared the long bridge. Carrie and Fritz walked on across, not even stopping to peer between the planks to watch the logs float toward the dam.

She wiped her forehead and tucked a damp strand of hair behind one ear. "It's hotter and the smoke is worse here than at home." She stopped and shifted the heavy basket.

Fritz pulled at her skirt, trying to make her hurry.

In the tavern across the street from the church men laughed and yelled.

"Why are they laughing?" asked Fritz with a frown.

"I don't know. Oma said noisy people in taverns aren't always happy people. They must not be worried about the fires." She took Fritz's hand and hurried across the busy street watching for horses and lumber carts. She looked at the sky. Gray smoke swirled slowly over her as though hiding some ugly secret.

A secret no one in the whole village knew.

Chapter 10 — *Father Pernin*

Carrie climbed the church steps. She pushed the heavy wooden door open. Fritz followed close behind her. It was a little cooler in the church.

"There's nothing here!" she exclaimed, setting the basket down. Then she remembered. Mr. Zutter, Lisa's father, would be plastering the walls this week. The pews built by Papa and others would be set into place later.

The unfinished building needed a lot of work but the congregation was so proud of their new church. And Father Pernin was proud of his parish, which he called his little flock of sheep. But Carrie knew some acted more like stubborn goats.

"Hello, my *kinder*." Father Pernin came toward them with his arms wide. His German, spoken with his French accent, made Carrie smile but she knew he was saying children. And Miss Moore's right, she thought. Americans do need English.

Americans! Carrie tasted the word. She felt like she belonged to a great big family every time she said it. She remembered every part of the ceremony that special day she and her family became American citizens.

Father Pernin motioned to some boxes. "Come. Sit and rest. You look so warm."

He sure doesn't look much like a priest in his coarse brown shirt and baggy pants, Carrie thought, as she perched on a box packed full of papers and books.

He sighed and wiped his damp face. "What brings you here on such a bad evening?"

"Mama sent some food. And she and Papa invite you to come to the farm where it is cooler."

"That is thoughtful of them, but I have work to do." Worry lines creased his round face. He picked up a stack of hymnals and started out the side door.

"We will help," called Carrie.

Fritz tugged at her skirt. "Mama said come home."

"Yes, I know, but we will help first."

"Put your kind gift of food in the house then come to the garden," Father Pernin called over his shoulder. As Carrie and Fritz came out of his house, several children were playing Kick the Can, laughing and pushing each other. Carrie wondered how they could be so happy.

Lisa ran up the steps, her ginger colored braids bobbing behind her. "Oh, isn't it dreadful? The smoke I mean." She rubbed her eyes.

Carrie nodded. "We're helping Father. Come on. Bring a box." Carrie picked up one and started out the door. "Lisa, come home with us."

"I can't. Mama is getting awfully nervous about the fires. She said I couldn't go anywhere while she is at Grandmother's in Marinette. And Papa went to our potato field north of town."

"Maybe you...that noise!" Carrie's eyes grew wide. "That rumbling in the west. Not even the locomotives ever sound like that!"

The girls ran behind the church. There was Father Pernin digging a long ditch in his garden. Faster and faster he swung a pickax over his head, then brought it down with all his strength.

"We—must—bury—the church records and books," he said, swinging the pickax with every word. He gripped it so hard the veins stood out on his big hands. Carrie knew his thick shirt was too warm. She wondered if he had any other work shirts. Probably not. Priests didn't have much money.

The girls left the boxes of papers next to the hole and ran back for more.

"Why bury them?" Lisa asked, putting another box near Father Pernin.

"Protect them from the fire."

Carrie felt fingers of fear move up her back.

Father Pernin continued to make the trench deeper.

The children continued to run back and forth carrying books and boxes. Even Fritz did his share without a whimper, knowing they were doing something very important.

At last the papers and books were buried deep and covered with sand.

Fritz dropped to the ground, rubbing his eyes. "Carrie! Let's go home," he wailed.

"Something awful is about to happen," Lisa whispered. "I can feel it."

"Get up, Fritz." Carrie helped him. "Let's go!"

But Father Pernin's hand squeezed her shoulder. "No." He looked up as thick black smoke rolled overhead. "There is no time."

He ran across the church yard to his carriage house and flung open the doors. Grabbing the bit and bridle he tried to slip it over his pony's head. But the gentle chestnut, always eager to take his master on parish visits, shook his head and refused the bit in his mouth.

Stepping aside Father Pernin slapped the pony on the rump. "Go, my faithful friend. You have a better chance without us." Then he stepped between the buggy shafts, gripped them and pulled the little cart to the church door. He raced inside, then came out carrying a white wooden box with little doors that opened. *The tabernacle*, thought Carrie. *With the Blessed Sacrament in it.*

A deer ran past her, then stopped as though it wasn't sure which way to run. But from what? Carrie couldn't see anything chasing it. Clouds boiled over the town like black-bean soup in a big pot. A throbbing red sky glowed in the west. Birds flew back and forth beneath the rolling smoke.

A low moan rose and fell across the heavens.

Father Pernin, his hand on the loaded buggy, looked up. "The wind. A strange wind."

"Yes, a *seltsam* wind," added Carrie. Suddenly she wished with all her heart she and Fritz were home with Mama and Papa.

Father Pernin gently brushed Fritz's curls out of his eyes. "Be brave, my children. God is with us."

Suddenly the sky blazed crimson and gold. The church bell across the river began to ring. "That's the signal," said Father Pernin. "It's coming!" The wind became so hot it took Carrie's breath.

People streamed from their homes like mice before a flood. The mill whistle gave a long blast.

Terrified, Fritz hooked his arms around Carrie. She couldn't move.

Father Pernin gathered the children to him. "Now listen carefully," he yelled over the roar of the wind. "Hold on to the buggy. Don't let go — no matter what happens." He started to open the gate of the church yard. Just then a violent gust of wind whipped the fence, gate and all, up in the air and over the trees.

With the way clear Father Pernin gripped the poles of the buggy, and leaning into the wind, started out onto the street.

People came running. Men staggered out of the tavern, confused. Some sat on the steps, not knowing what to do. Women and children clutched bedding, clothing — whatever they could carry. A man bumped into Carrie. He had a rocking chair strapped to his back. Everyone had one thought. Get to the river!

Chapter 11 — *To the River*

Agust of hot wind tore at Carrie's skirt. She clutched the side of the buggy with one hand and held on to Fritz with the other. *Two blocks to the river!* Carrie tried to open her eyes. Tears blinded her. *Oh, why didn't we go home?*

She gasped for breath but the hot air, swirling sand, and ashes stung her face. She squeezed her eyes tight and hoped Father Pernin could see the way. She clung to the buggy so hard her hand hurt. Someone slammed into her side. She staggered and almost fell. A small two-wheel cart piled high with chairs and a bed tipped over. The old man pulling it stopped to upright it.

A boy pushed his way to the old man and started to lift the cart.

Father Pernin shouted, "No! Come on!" He shoved them along in the mob.

That's Hans Heiss, Carrie thought. Helping an old man? That can't be!

People ran out of their houses from both sides of the street. A woman balanced a feather mattress on her head. The wind howled with sounds never heard before. The mattress was jerked from the woman's hands and rolled end over end.

Carrie threw her skirt over Fritz's head as he followed close behind, one hand on the wagon and one clenched around Carrie's arm.

A young woman holding a rag over her nose came toward them pushing her way against the crowd. She called for her children. Father Pernin tried to turn her around but she pulled away from him.

Fritz stumbled. He turned loose of Carrie and slid to the ground. She grabbed for him but the buggy pulled her on. She screamed at Father Pernin and pointed to Fritz.

Father Pernin stopped, scooped Fritz up and put him in the buggy. On they went. Carrie slammed against a wagon that was lying upside down, its wheels still turning.

Lisa clung to the other side of the buggy with one hand over her face to shut out swirling sand that bit into her cheeks. A dog barked close to Carrie but she couldn't see it.

"Kleine! I hear Kleine!" Fritz yelled in Carrie's ear.

"No," she screamed. "It can't be."

Father Pernin found an opening in the mob. He began to run, glancing over his shoulder to see that the children were still with him.

Carrie knew she had never felt anything like this. Not even when she pushed with all her might against the stone boat filled with rocks. Her legs screamed for her to stop.

"Keep running!" Father Pernin commanded over his shoulder.

"Where's the bridge?" Carrie yelled. But no one could hear her. The fire roared and swirled overhead ready to swoop down and swallow everything in its path.

Carrie didn't see the runaway horse and empty wagon bearing down on them. The wagon struck the buggy, throwing Carrie and Lisa to the ground. Carrie coughed and gagged as ash and sand filled her mouth.

"Get up!" Father Pernin yelled.

Carrie forced her face out of the dirt and opened her eyes. She could see the bridge! With her last strength she pulled herself up. Father Pernin dropped the buggy poles, grabbed the girls and pushed them forward so hard that only their tip-toes touched the big rough planks as they ran.

Father Pernin raced back and pulled the buggy down the river bank and straight into the deep water.

Fritz, still on the buggy seat next to the tabernacle, lifted his arms to Carrie. She could see the terror in his face. He opened his mouth to scream for her, but the waters closed over him.

In the middle of the bridge Carrie clung to the rail, gasping for breath.

Clouds of fire dipped, turned and twisted in eerie shapes. The Congregational church steeple exploded into flames. Taverns and houses became torches lighting the sky. Carrie wanted to wake up. It had to be one of her worst dreams. Oh, to pull her crazy quilt over her head. She buried her head against Lisa's back.

With the roar of a cannon, a ball of fire hit the bridge railing. It burst into flame and tumbled into the water. The whole bridge was burning. Fire crackled and leaped around Carrie's feet.

"Everybody jump! Jump!" Someone called. Screams filled the air. For an instant Carrie felt a cool breeze on her cheeks. She gasped, "Is that you, God?" Then the words that Father Pernin read in church came to her. "When you pass through the waters I will be with you...the flames will not set you ablaze."

Carrie grabbed Lisa around the waist and stepped over the edge of the bridge. Lisa's scream was in her ear as they plunged into the black water below.

Chapter 12 — *Carrie and the Cow*

There was no time to think about the dark cold water. Terror swallowed Carrie as she plunged to the bottom of the river. Mud sucked at her bare toes. She pushed upward with all her might. She kicked and fought. Oh, to get out of the blackness. Suddenly her head shot above water. She gulped air. Bitter cold turned to blistering heat.

Flames shot back and forth all around her. No Lisa! Pieces of the bridge fell into the water with hisses greater than the biggest engine in the mill.

Fire swept across Carrie's hair. Down she went to escape. Up. Down. Up. Down again. She bobbed without counting. She heard her own gasps.

Just quit trying, a voice in her head said. No! She wouldn't give up. She wouldn't.

A log, slippery and cold, floated next to her. She threw her arm over it. It began to roll and got away from her. A plank slammed against her. Before she could grasp it, it slipped away. Within her another voice, a soft quiet voice said, *Don't give up, Carrie. I am with you always.*

Suddenly a woman next to her screamed and grabbed Carrie's hair, trying to climb upon her shoulders. She pushed Carrie under. Carrie wanted to fight her way to the surface. But she let herself sink. It worked. The woman let go and grabbed a box floating by.

Carrie sucked in air. *Oh, help me! Please help me, God. Please – please help me!*

A wall of thick inky smoke dropped down over the river. Towering flames – orange, yellow, and red, danced around her. Her eyes hurt so. She squeezed them tight. Her hand closed over something smooth and round. She held on.

Oh, Lisa! Where are you?

Something bumped against her. Something big and hairy. A terrible sound filled the air.

"M-o-o-o-o!"

A cow? I'm holding a cow's horn.

The big hooves churned the water, inches from her legs. Carrie pushed away as far as she could but the river pushed her against the cow again. *Will she hurt me? Like Hildy tried to do?*

The head, as big as Mama's washtub, it seemed to Carrie, was only inches from her face. The cow snorted and shook her head, flinging her unwanted passenger loose. Carrie grabbed a floating timber, but it sank. She tread water. Her legs had no feeling. So cold! Icy cold.

The cow was there again. Next to her! *Does she really want to be near me? Like Hildy when we walk together to the barn?*

Carefully, Carrie reached out and took hold of the horn again. She waited. The cow was quiet except for blubbering snorting sounds when her big nose went under water.

"You don't want to be alone either, do you?" Carrie whispered through chattering teeth.

The cow turned toward the middle of the river taking Carrie with her. Away from the burning bridge. Away from the biting heat. Away from the noise and the flames that flashed around her.

Carrie's numb fingers began to slip from the cow's horn. She reached up to slide her arm over the wide back. "Oh, no! You're on fire!" She cupped her hands and threw water. Over and over. Even though pain tore at her arms she wouldn't quit until the cow's back and head were soaking wet.

Then Carrie felt the burning pain in her own head. Under she went and stayed as long as she could before coming up gasping for air, her teeth chattering.

She leaned against the broad side. "Are you someone's pet, like Hildy?" she whispered into the big soft ear. "I will pretend you are my Hildy."

It felt good to talk even though her throat was sore from the smoke. It helped shut out the fear. Fear that choked her even more than the smoke. "Maybe God brought you to me. He knows how scared I am. And he knows how scared you are, too."

Something slithered across her knees and coiled around her ankle. A snake? Carrie held her breath. Slowly it uncoiled and came to the surface. It slid against her cheek. She jerked away but it touched her again. She hit it as hard as she could.

"A rope! It's only a rope. Oh, Hildy, it's just a rope." She sobbed. When she pulled it the cow's nose bumped her face.

"It's your halter rope." The cow became quiet as Carrie continued to talk to her. Now they were far out from shore. A pocket of sweet air clung near the top of the water. Carrie breathed in the coolness. With her head against the cow's shoulder her eyes grew heavy.

She was so tired — so cold. So awfully cold.

Chapter 13 — *Together Again*

Fire and smoke blended to create black destruction over the river.

Strange ideas rambled around in Carrie's head. "If only I had my crazy quilt we would be warm, Hildy. Mama, I'm so sorry I didn't come home."

How long had she been in the river? She remembered what happened on the bridge just before she and Lisa jumped. *When thou passest through the waters, I will be with thee...*

"That's from the Bible, Hildy, and it means God is with us right now!" It was hard to believe the words. But she would believe! Her teeth chattered. Her eyes burned. She hugged close to the cow's thick neck, trying to find warmth. She stroked Hildy's nose. They were away from the crying people huddled along the bank who were too afraid of water to get in the river.

Suddenly a thunderous roar filled the air. Carrie gulped air and went under water. Seltsam! What now?

She came up. The woodenware factory! Kegs of varnish and paint were exploding, spewing out splintered wood and sheets of fire. The building was a giant flare against the sky. The river was as bright as noon. Carrie could see people up and down the river, clutching boxes, logs, anything that would float.

"Carrie — Carrie — Carrie."

Carrie twisted around straining to see behind her. She almost lost her grip on Hildy's horn. Was she really hearing her name?

"Carrie! Oh, where are you?"

"Lisa? Is it you? Is it really you?"

Lisa, hanging onto a wooden wash tub, bumped against Hildy's cold hairy side. "WHAT'S THAT?" She jerked away.

"A cow. And she's scared. Just like us. Oh Lisa, it *is* you. I thought — I thought you were — gone."

Lisa tried to stay away from Hildy. "A cow? Are you sure?" She pushed away, clinging to the tub as it bobbed in the water.

"Yes, a cow. Just like my Hildy. Here. Touch her. She won't hurt you."

Carefully Lisa moved closer to the cow to be with Carrie. The girls huddled together.

"What's this?" Carrie asked, feeling something thick and soggy hanging out of the tub. "Oh, it's a quilt! Let's pull it over us."

"Be careful," Lisa warned. "There's a baby in it. I grabbed hold of the tub after we jumped from the bridge."

"Baby? A real live baby?"

"Wrapped in a corner of the quilt," Lisa explained.

Carrie felt around in the big tub. A baby wiggled in the rolls of heavy quilt. "Help me get a corner of the quilt through the tub handles. We'll make a tent."

They tugged and pulled at the heavy wet quilt, poking it through the holes that formed handles in the tub made of slabs held together with iron bands.

Suddenly there were more explosions in the woodenware factory and fire swept over the river again. Carrie and Lisa went under water. At last the quilt was over the tub and over the cow's back forming a wet tent. The baby, still wrapped, didn't cry. The river gently rocked the tub cradle.

Firelight danced on the quilt. Carrie stared at it. "Lisa!" she cried. "I know this baby."

"How?"

"This quilt," Carrie said touching it to her cheek. "Yes. This is the crazy quilt Oma and I made for the church raffle. Frieda Zahn won it. Remember?"

"You think the baby is Anita Zahn?"

"I know she is! This is the quilt!"

Carrie would know it anywhere. She and Oma worked on it many evenings. And how many times had she ripped stitches that Oma decided were not small enough? It made Carrie think of her old crazy quilt on her bed at home. She rubbed the edge of the quilt between her fingers. *Oma – Oma – Oma.*

"Ach!" Lisa exclaimed, coming out from under the quilt tent. "What's that awful sound?"   •

Carrie peered out. Clean cold air filled her lungs.

"What's happening?" Lisa whispered.

The noise made Carrie think of her Hildy drinking at the creek. Sucking with her thick muzzle. Only this was louder—a thousand times louder. They watched in awe as hot air from the fire and cold air over the river mixed, forming a whirlwind that sucked smoke up high over the river.

"*Seltsam!*" Carrie watched in awe.

The whirlwind continued to pull the smoke skyward. The girls gulped air as delicious and cool as at the spring.

Through swollen eyes caused by the smoke, Carrie could see where stores and houses had been only a few hours earlier. She saw a man on the river bank. He rushed back and forth pulling people into the water to escape the flames. His shirt was gone. His trousers hung in burned tatters. He stopped only to get in the water and go under for a few seconds.

"Father Pernin!" Carrie exclaimed. "It's me, Carrie!" At the sound of his name, he searched the mass of people. "Carrie! Thank God you are safe. Stay where you are!" He ducked under but soon came up and continued to help others.

Carrie cupped her hands and called as loud as her sore throat would let her. "Where's Fritz?"

Father Pernin shook his head.

Didn't he hear her? Or did he mean...? Gone? Fritz gone? Carrie pressed her head against Hildy and sobbed.

The girls didn't see the log bobbing and wobbling along behind them. It struck Carrie behind one ear. Lights blinked in her head. Pain shut out all sound. Her hand opened. She let go of Hildy's horn. Carrie began to sink.

Chapter 14 — *The Long Night*

"M-A-A-A-A-W! M-O-O-O!" Hildy bawled. The sound rolled up and down the river.

Carrie jerked her head above water. *What was that?* She gasped and coughed trying to breathe. She had swallowed a lot of water.

Hildy bumped against her. With trembling fingers Carrie inched her way along Hildy's side until she was safe under the blanket again. She coughed again and again.

"Carrie? What's wrong? What happened?" Lisa peered under Hildy's neck from the other side.

"I'm all right," she managed to answer. She touched a large lump behind her ear. If only her head would stop hurting so she could think.

A burning log floated against Hildy. The cow turned and swam upstream to get away from it, carrying her strange load of passengers with her.

A door, blown off the woodenware factory, floated by. A child whimpered. Carrie forced her eyes open. Oh, how they burned. She squeezed them tight. If only the pain in her head would go away.

Carrie's only thought was to hang on to Hildy and the quilt. She remembered Oma's words. *Carrie, my Liebling, life is like this crazy quilt....*

If only morning would come.

"Help. Please help me," someone near Carrie called.

"I can't," Carrie replied.

"Who are you?"

"Carrie Heidenworth."

"Caroline?"

Carrie lifted the crazy quilt and squinted.

A woman had her arms around a little keg that bobbed up and down. Carrie reached out and pulled it toward her. Even though the long dark hair was singed close to her head Carrie knew. The woman was her teacher, Miss Moore.

"Oh, help me." She grabbed Carrie and almost pulled her under.

"Here." Carrie guided her trembling hand to Hildy and pulled the quilt over her.

"It's the end of the world." Miss Moore sobbed softly, too afraid to notice she was leaning against a cow.

Miss Moore afraid? Carrie pulled the quilt to cover her teacher's back. *She's young, not much older than me, Carrie suddenly realized.*

Since her father was the steamboat captain, Miss Moore's clothes were nicer than the other two teachers at the school. The tight french braid across her head never had a hair out of place, no matter how hot the day. And her curly long hair was always as shiny as Mama's silk shawl.

Carrie thought, *She's even more afraid than I am. Maybe she's scared when she scolds Hans Heiss and the other big boys.*

"This fire wasn't caused by God," Carrie said. "Locomotives. Burning stumps. They cause fires." And she was surprised to know that she believed what she was saying. She moved a little closer to her teacher. "And I know that if I die I'll be in Heaven."

"But I don't want to die," Miss Moore sobbed.

"I don't think we'll die. God is taking care of us. He gave us this cow—and this quilt."

"You are so brave, Carrie. I'm a coward."

Brave? How could she think I'm brave? I'm a feigling. Carrie clutched her necklace as tight as her numb fingers would let her.

Miss Moore moved closer to Carrie. "I think I'm going to die," she whispered.

Carrie didn't know what to say. And she was so tired...so very tired. But she would stay awake. She had to because she knew. Yes, Carrie knew. Morning would come.

Chapter 15 — *Rescued*

T he door, blown off the woodenware factory, was not far from Carrie. It was caught in a jumble of logs. But Carrie didn't see it. And she didn't see the little boy in Father Pernin's big baggy shirt, lying face down on the door.

"Kleine!" the boy called.

Carrie knew that voice! She threw back the quilt. The door came almost within her reach. Then the logs and door began to move again. They floated toward the spillway, at one end of the dam, where water tumbled through a narrow opening to the river below.

"That's my little brother."

"Go get him," Miss Moore urged.

"I—I can't see." She squinted. Everything looked cloudy.

"You can do it," Lisa urged from the other side of Hildy.

Carrie took a deep breath and let go of Hildy. A burning log floated in front of her. She grabbed

Hildy's horn again. She blinked, trying to see. The door stopped, then moved again. But it was backing up against the flow of the river.

"*Seltsam!*" How can it do that?" Carrie exclaimed.

Now it floated toward the dam again. The spillway, a wide-jawed monster, was swallowing everything that came near. The logs, the door, and Fritz would be next.

Almost without thinking Carrie put her feet against Hildy's belly, took a deep breath and pushed with all her might. Just like she pushed off from Bear Rock so many times.

With her face down and her arms straight in front of her she shot through the water. She bumped against the door. Her hands grabbed the thick soggy shirt on Fritz.

An animal, bigger than a beaver, had the edge of the door in its teeth trying to pull it upstream. *Whatever you are, you won't get my little bruder.* Carrie pulled as hard as she could. But the animal held on. It began to whine, begging for Carrie's help.

"Kleine? Kleine! Good dog!"

The collie pulled again.

Carrie tried to help him but suddenly the door flipped over. Fritz was gone! The door zig-zagged through the spillway and dropped out of sight.

Kleine came up holding the heavy shirt between his strong jaws. Fritz was in it but his head and shoulders were under water. As Carrie reached for him the pain in her head poured all through her.

Someone swam next to her. A strong hand gripped her shoulder holding her up. The other held Fritz by the shirt and pulled his head above water.

"Come on, Carrie. Ya' gotta' help me," commanded the gruff voice next to her. "I can't hold him and you too."

She tried to think.

"Kick. Come on. You gotta' swim or I can't hang on to him."

In spite of her pain Carrie began to swim slowly toward Hildy with Kleine near her side.

The cow bawled and swam in circles to stay away from the dog.

"Hildy! It's okay. We need you." Hearing Carrie's voice the cow turned toward her.

"You're talkin' to a dumb cow."

"Not a dumb cow," she mumbled through her pain.

The stranger took the rope and tied Fritz to Hildy's side. Lisa pulled a corner of the quilt over him.

"Hildy, my foot," said the voice. "Just a dumb cow who is afraid of the fire and afraid of your dog."

"Who are you?" Carrie demanded.

"You don't know? I'm glad you ain't got your lunch bucket. I still remember when you smacked me with it."

"Hans Heiss? You? You helped me? Why?"

"That's a dumb question." He clenched his teeth to keep them from chattering. "We gotta' help everybody."

"You—helped—us," Carrie repeated fighting the pain in her head. "You saved my little brother's life."

"Aw, Carrie. I know I was the worst guy in school, but—but I'm different. And not just because of this fire that's got us scared to death."

"What is it?"

"You don't wanna' know."

"Yes, I do." She still couldn't believe Hans Heiss would talk to her like this. And she thought he was so mean. She forgot about her pain. She forgot how cold she was. It was good to talk.

The quilt began to steam again from the heat. She reached to splash water on it. Hans helped her.

"Well, after I got punished for breaking a window in the new school—yeah, I broke a window. Just foolin' around. Anyway, part of my punishment was to clean up the school yard."

Carrie remembered. She had seen him from the wagon on her way to church that Sunday morning.

"Somehow, I knew that new school was important—real important." He stopped and shook his head. "But it doesn't matter now. It's all burnt up. There ain't gonna' be no school. Nobody can learn to read now."

Carrie hurt too much to argue with him but she knew he was wrong. There would be a school again someday.

"Anyway," he continued, "I want—I want to be somebody."

"And you will be, with God's help," Carrie said.

"God?" Hans replied.

Carrie knew Miss Moore would be surprised to know Hans Heiss had changed—had really changed.

"Lisa, where is Miss Moore?"

"I thought she was there," replied Lisa.

Where could she be? Carrie wanted to call to her but the pain in her head took over again. She clung to Hildy.

"You okay?" Hans asked. He took her arm and held tight.

Chapter 16 — *A New Day*

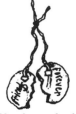arrie listened. People called and shouted to one another up and down the river.

"I can see the sun!"

"Me too! There it is!"

Carrie strained to see but she couldn't. Even though the horrible roar of the fire was gone, burning timber still hissed round her. A man called for his family. No one answered him.

The remains of the village lay in black lumps. Curls of smoke threaded their way up through the rays of the rising sun.

Carrie leaned against Hildy and wished she didn't hurt so.

Hans rubbed Hildy's side. "You're okay, old cow. I'm glad you let me join this bunch hangin' on to you."

Carrie was glad too. "Lisa, are you there?"

"Yes, and I can see the sun!"

Kleine whimpered.

"Come here, boy," Hans called.

The weary dog swam toward him.

"Here." Hans grasped his soggy fur. "Don't give up. You can't give up now!" He pushed a long stick under the dog's chin so he could rest his head and paws on it. Now his head was above water.

Hildy, nervous with the dog so near, started to swim away.

"Hildy, go to shore," Carrie commanded, as though the cow understood her. But Hildy swam in circles, then turned toward the middle of the river.

Carrie put her arm over the cow's back. "Please help us, God. I'm so tired. And I can't see the river bank."

"I can."

"Fritz? What did you say?"

"I can see the river bank." He pushed the quilt away. "There's Father Pernin. He sees us."

"Can you keep Hildy's head turned toward him?" Carrie asked.

Fritz tugged at the rope halter.

"I'll help," Hans said. He swam to the front of the cow. "Come on, Hildy. Let's get out of this cold water." Hans pulled the rope but Hildy tried to turn back. Then she tried to swim upstream. But Hans and Carrie wouldn't let her have her way.

At last they were on the bank.

Carrie's feet sank in the cold mud of the river's edge. But her legs couldn't hold her up. She let go of Hildy, dropped to the ground, and crawled. The sand was almost too hot against her shivering body. The warmth flooded her aching legs and knees.

Hans, with his arm around Fritz, stretched out on the sand gasping for breath from pulling and tugging at the cow's rope.

Hildy clumped up the steep bank with her strange burden clinging to her. The wooden tub bounced back and forth. Lisa wiggled free of the rope and sank down next to the others.

Father Pernin watched. His face was as black as his ragged pants. He took the quilt and tub from the cow's side. Blood oozed from his burned bald head.

"What's this? A child?" He gently removed the baby, still wrapped in a corner of the crazy quilt and put her on the warm sand next to Lisa.

"It's Anita Zahn," said Lisa.

Carrie inched her way to a burning log and soaked in its warmth. If only she could see. She tried to take a deep breath. But the smoke made her cough and choke.

Slowly she scooped sand over her legs. She started to push her singed hair behind her ears but stopped and jerked her hand back. Carefully she touched her head where her hair should have been. A mass of blisters covered her head like huge bee stings.

"No! No!" She cried. "Gone! My hair. It's gone!"

The bump behind her ear was bigger than before.

"Father?" she called.

"Yes, child," he answered quietly.

"My hair. It's gone. And I can't see. I'm blind!" She bit her lip so she wouldn't scream.

He squeezed her shoulder gently. "I know. Smoke blindness. You'll see again."

But his voice didn't convince her.

Gently he took his shirt off of Fritz and wrung it out. He put it on a long stick and held it over the burning log.

Fritz curled next to Carrie. She pulled him close and wrapped him in her arms. "It's over, little bruder. It's over, over, over, and we are alive." She sang the words, making them a soft lullaby.

Fritz sighed. Sobs jerked his thin chest. He fell asleep clutching Carrie's hand.

Carrie, Fritz, Hans, Lisa and the baby slept soundly as the sun moved across the sky, dimmed by blankets of gray-black smoke.

Kleine, his golden coat tangled and scorched, licked Fritz's hand. The weary dog stretched out on the hot sand with his blistered nose on Fritz's leg. At last his young master was safe.

Fritz stirred. "Let's we go home," he mumbled.

Lisa slept, curled up near Carrie with the baby close to her.

"Help will come," Father Pernin said as he sat nearby. "Let's pray it comes soon."

"Father Pernin!" An old man called as he hobbled toward them. "Look!" He pointed to a snowy white box on a burned log at the river's edge.

"The tabernacle!" Father Pernin knelt and gently opened the small door. There lay the ciborium, a bowl shaped container for the communion bread. The silky lining of the tabernacle wasn't scorched. How can this be?" he whispered.

It's a miracle, that's what it is," said the old man.

"Carrie!" A young woman hobbled toward them, her lace blouse hanging in shreds over her camisole.

This time Carrie knew that voice. She tried to get up.

Miss Moore sat next to Carrie and took her hands in hers. "You are safe. And your very special friend Hildy, too." She reached up and patted the cow who stood patiently waiting for Carrie.

"We thought you...How did you...?" Carrie couldn't finish.

"I don't know." She said each word slowly. " I truly don't. I was so afraid." She rubbed her hands together. "I remember praying. I told God that whatever happened I would trust Him." She looked at the water, black with soot, and trash. "Then it was morning and I was sitting on the sand. My feet were still in the river." She leaned over and gave Carrie a gentle hug, careful not to touch her blistered arms. "Your faith and courage were with me."

Carrie didn't know what to say.

"I must go now and find my father's boat. I'm sure he navigated out into the bay and is safe." She looked at the rubble which only yesterday was a town. "I'll be living in Marinette for awhile."

"I'll miss you," Carrie said.

Miss Moore struggled to stand up. "She put her hands on Carrie's cheeks. "I can't thank you enough. I wonder what God wants me to do now?" Her voice was soft and calm.

Hans had been listening. He moved closer to Carrie and started to say something. Then he shook his head, turned and walked away.

Chapter 18 — *Blessings*

The baby kicked the quilt off and began to cry. Lisa picked her up and cuddled her close to her. She ran her fingers gently across her tiny forehead. "You're hungry. So am I."

"Carrie," Father asked, "can you milk that cow?"

"I don't think she will have any milk after being so scared. But I would try if I had a cup or pail." Then she thought of something. She tore the ruffle from her petticoat. "Hildy, we still need you. This baby is hungry — we all are." She reached up and patted the cow's side. Hildy stood quietly while Carrie milked.

Carrie couldn't believe it. Milk! Good rich milk! "Thank you, Hildy." She soaked the cloth and handed it to Lisa. The baby sucked it eagerly and cried for more. After several times she was full and fell asleep in Lisa's lap. "I'm hungry, too," said Fritz. "Here, cup your hands like this." Carrie milked. "Now drink it quick before it leaks through your fingers."

Everyone took turns.

"Any for me?" Hans asked as he returned to the group.

"I think so," said Carrie. He's different. His voice is nice.

"Now your turn," Hans told her and took her place. The warm milk soothed her throat, so sore from the smoke. Never had anything tasted so good.

"Carrie, I..." Hans began.

"Hello there!" A tall thin man interrupted. His voice was weak. His shirt and pants were caked with dried mud. He carried a bucket of potatoes. "Has anyone seen my little girl? She's ten years old and has..."

Lisa struggled to stand. "Papa!" she screamed. "Oh, Papa." She threw her arms around him.

He dropped the bucket and picked her up. "Lisa! My little Lisa!" She snuggled close to him without a thought about the mud.

He gave everyone a potato.

Carrie bit into hers and rolled the chunk around in her mouth. "Seltsam! It's—it's cooked!"

"Yes, strange, indeed," said Father Pernin.

"Cooked by the heat in the ground," explained Mr. Zutter. "From the fire."

"God does provide," exclaimed Father Pernin. "Tell me, Mr. Zutter, how did you survive?" He looked at the muddy clothes. "You weren't in the river."

"No. In a pond in my potato field. I was there when the fire swooped down like something from Hell itself. Never have I seen such a sight."

He swallowed to calm his trembling voice. "And I pray to Gott in Heaven that I never see it again. I stretched out flat in that pond. But the fire dried it up. I rolled in the mud, just like a hog." He squeezed Lisa close. "I worried about my Lisa and my wife all night." He put her down gently. "And now you're both safe."

"Where is Mama?" asked Lisa. Then she remembered. "Oh, yes. At grandmother's in Marinette."

Mr. Zutter looked toward Heaven. "I thank der liebe Gott—a loving God. And now to find my little Lisa safe." He stopped. Tears filled his eyes. "It's almost too much."

Lisa clung to his hand as though afraid of losing him again.

"Come along, my *Liebling*." He put his arm around her.

Lisa picked up the baby. "Papa, this is Frieda Zahn's baby."

"Bring the little one along. We'll try to find the Zahns."

"Lisa," said Carrie, "I have my necklace. Just like they say, FRIENDS FOREVER."

"And I have mine, too," Lisa replied. She stood and looked around. "I'll miss you all. Goodbye."

Carrie listened as Lisa walked away talking to her Papa. *When would she ever see her again?*

Chapter 19 — *Waiting*

F ather Pernin stood up to stretch some of the stiffness from his weary body. "I'll ask if anyone knows when help will come."

Carrie touched her scalp, careful not to break the blisters. It stung even worse than her arms.

"Carrie." Hans sat down beside her. "Can I talk to you?"

She nodded. *Why did he sound so strange?*

"I heard what Miss Moore told you." He stopped and made circles in the sand with a stick. "My...I had something happen too. I — that is, Jesus made it happen."

She could feel him squirming next to her. How she wished she could see his face.

"I mean — I'm not the same. God did something."

She leaned forward. "Please tell me."

"In the river. Before I found you — you and that cow. I was so scared. I couldn't even swim. I couldn't do nothin.' Then it happened."

"What? What are you talking about?" But Carrie was sure she knew.

"You gotta' believe me. Will you believe me?"

"Believe what?"

"Jesus was there. There in the water by me. Oh, I didn't *see* Him. But He was there! You gotta' believe me."

"I believe you," she answered quietly, "because He was with me, too. He talked to me on the bridge, just before I jumped off."

"Really?"

"I think it happened to a lot of people," Carrie continued. "That's the way God is, you know. He can be everywhere at once." She stopped. "Hans, what did he say to you?"

"Say? Nothing. He was just there. And you know something? He's here now." His voice dropped to a whisper. "Everything is goin' be okay."

"*I will never leave you nor forsake you,*" Carrie said.

"What?"

"That's what the Bible says. Oma — my grandmother — used to read it to me."

"Carrie, people will say we were so scared we just *thought* this happened. Let's not tell nobody."

"Anybody," Carrie corrected him without thinking.

"Right. Anybody — nobody."

"Well, let's pray," she said. "Let's ask God if we should tell."

Hans made more marks in the sand with his stick. "I don't know nothin' — anything — about praying."

"It's just talking to God. Like we're talking here now."

Father Pernin returned telling everyone that help was on the way from Oconto and Marinette. "Don't give up!" he called. "Wagons with food and blankets are coming. Doctors, too."

He sat down next to Carrie. "They'll be here in the morning. The roads have to be cleared of burning trees."

Fritz woke up. "I want to go home."

Father Pernin put Fritz on his lap. "That's not possible, son." He put his arm around Carrie's shoulder. "I must tell you something."

Carrie didn't like the sound of his voice. If only she could see his face.

"You and Fritz will go to Oconto. You will have—a home—and family there."

Carrie jerked away from him. "Home? But we have a home," she snapped. "Here on the..." She stopped. "Family? What—about—Mama and Papa?" Suddenly she knew. She pressed her hand over her mouth so she wouldn't scream.

"There are no survivors around your homestead," he answered. "Not one."

"But they took blankets and went to the creek! Papa told me they would."

"Not enough time."

"Where are Mama and Papa?" asked Fritz.

Hans took Fritz from Father Pernin. "Come on, let's go find more of those good potatoes."

"Thank you, Hans." Father Pernin said.

Carrie lay down and buried her face in her hands. Father Pernin covered her with the crazy quilt which had dried on the warm sand.

Carrie cried until she fell asleep.

Chapter 20 – *Help Arrives*

T he next morning a parade of wagons pulled into town.

"It was a slow 12 miles," said the lead driver. "Even with all the men from the Oconto sawmill clearing the road. It still took all night."

Carrie lay looking at the cloudy sky. So beautiful! She could see! Everything was fuzzy but she could see. "Oh, thank you God," she whispered.

"Can Mama and Papa really be gone?" And the homestead, too?

She listened to Fritz's quiet breathing next to her. She knew it really happened. This was not one of her bad dreams. *Mama – Papa – they were gone.* But she knew that she would see them again. And Oma and Grandfather, too.

*I will never leave you nor forsake you...*that verse again. She sat up and looked around. Nothing was the same. Nothing. And it would never be like it was. Not ever again. But she also knew that fear could never smother her like it a did before the fire.

One of the men from the wagons came toward her. He blinked back tears as he knelt to help her.

Hans and Fritz came downstream. "Found some more potatoes," called Hans. "And watered the cow, too. Boy, was she thirsty. Right, Hil— old cow?"

The man patted the cow. "You've all been through so much."

Carrie managed to stand on shaky legs. She put her arms around Hildy's neck. "I have to go now. Thanks for being my friend."

"I'll take good care of her," said Hans.

"And Kleine? What about our dog?"

"And Kleine, too." Hans patted the weary dog's head. "He likes me."

Suddenly Carrie realized she hadn't asked him about his family. "Did you find your folks?"

He shrugged his shoulders. "I ain't got none. But I found my Uncle Auggie and Aunt Hettie. They'll sure be glad to have this cow." He rubbed the big ears gently. "Come on with me, old cow."

"Her name's Hildy," Carrie corrected him.

Hans grinned. "Hildy." He started to lead the cow away, then stopped. "Me and Hildy will come to Oconto to see you."

"You will?" asked Carrie surprised. "You and Hildy? To Oconto?"

"Sure."

"I suppose you're going to bridle her and ride her like a plow horse."

"Why not?"

She knew he was teasing. "I'm glad you'll come." She clutched the crazy quilt. Wherever she would go, it would be with her. She picked at some of the holes burned in it. She would patch them.

The wagon driver waited until all goodbyes were said then he helped Carrie and Fritz into the wagon with several others also going to Oconto.

Carrie snuggled Fritz close to her and pulled the crazy quilt over them.

Fritz whimpered.

"It's all right, little *bruder*. We'll be back." She stroked his cheek gently. "Yes, some day we'll come back to our homestead."

GLOSSARY

Ach!: Ah! Oh!
Bruder: Brother
Der Liebe Gott: The loving God
Feigling: Coward
Ja!: Yes
Kleine: Little, Small
Kinder: Children
Kommen Sie hier: Come here
Liebling: Favorite one, Pet
Mitkommen: Come along
Oma: Grandma
Opa: Grandpa
Seltsam: Strange, Odd

AUTHOR

Nelda Johnson Liebig's interest in history leads her to write stories of interesting people who lived long ago. Her historical stories are in magazines and elementary text books.

She taught elementary school in Alaska. Her Eskimo students had never seen cows, horses, or other farm animals so she wrote stories about village life and animals of the area. She taught English in American Samoa, a group of islands in the South Pacific Ocean. She wrote stories about village life for her elementary students.

Liebig was born in Oklahoma. Her faith in God has helped her through some bad times including a fire in her home when she was three years old. During a tornado, when she was fourteen, she and her mother guided several school children into the farm cellar as the storm approached.

She lives in Oconto, Wisconsin, near the site of the Peshtigo Fire. She and her husband have three grown children. She is an active member of First American Lutheran church of Oconto, Wisconsin, where she is a Bible study leader.

Liebig leads the Oconto Writers League. She also speaks to elementary classes to encourage students to develop their writing skills.

ILLUSTRATOR

Elizabeth Merryfield is a graduate of the University of Wisconsin. Her work includes holiday crafts and illustrating newsletters. She received an award in the 1979 *Wisconsin State Journal* art contest. She lives in Ozawkie, Kansas where she and her husband are wildflower enthusiasts and have landscaped their rural home with native Kansas plants.